This Storybook Belongs to:

Princess CHRISTA

Beauty and the Beast

Together Forever

Advance PUBLISHERS

Everyone at the castle was happy now that Belle and the Prince were married. The newlyweds were in love and enjoying their new life together. The servants were back to their human forms and looking after the household with care and efficiency. Phillipe, Belle's beloved horse, was living in a stable fit for a king—and, to Belle's delight, he had made a new friend, too!

So Belle was especially surprised to find Phillipe moping one morning when she brought him his breakfast.

"What's the matter, boy?" she asked with concern. "Aren't you feeling well?" Phillipe's tail drooped as he lowered his head and nuzzled Belle's hand.

"All right, then," she said, "let's have a look at you." Belle checked the horse over carefully, but he didn't appear to be sick or injured. "I'll be back later," she said, gently patting his side. "Don't worry. We'll figure out what's wrong with you and have you as good as new in no time."

Back inside the castle, Belle shared Phillipe's condition with Lumiere, Cogsworth, and Chip.

"Everyone loses his *joie de vivre* sometime," said Lumiere.

"What's '*joie de vivre*' mean?" Chip asked.

"His joy for life," Belle replied. "But how can we help him get it back?"

"Oh, that's easy!" exclaimed Belle's friends—though each one had a different solution in mind. Then they each recalled what had cheered them during the dark days when the castle had been under a spell.

"All it took to give me back my 'ooh la la' was a lively show with dancing and singing and costumes!" announced Lumiere.

"What about a concert?" asked Cogsworth. "Classical music can lift the spirits of any creature, man or beast!"

"When I wanted to feel better, I took a bath," Chip piped up. "There's nothing more fun than bubbles. You can watch them float. You can pop them. You can even see rainbows in them if you look hard enough!"

"Thank you," said Belle. "Anything is worth a try!"

The next morning she and Lumiere went out to the stables.
"Bonjour, mon amis!" said Lumiere cheerfully to Phillipe.
"Don't look so glum. Today we're going to put on a play! We have a beautiful stage and costumes galore, so . . . what should our play be about?"

But Phillipe just stared out the window, without so much as glancing in Lumiere's direction.

"How about a play about a brave horse who saves a damsel in distress?" asked Belle. "Or one about a horse who is the most loyal friend in all the world?"

With that, Phillipe hung his head even lower.

"Oh, dear," fretted Belle. "This isn't working at all."

"But a concert will," said Cogsworth, appearing in the
doorway. Chip poked his head in. "Can I watch, too?" he asked?
"Of course, the more the merrier," Cogsworth replied.
Soon lovely music filled the stable to the rafters. But when
Cogsworth looked over at Phillipe, the horse just stood morosely
munching on his program.

Chip leaned over and whispered in Belle's ear, then slipped out the door. After the concert was over, he stood waiting outside the stable.

"I've got a surprise for you, Phillipe!" Chip announced excitedly. "Follow me!"

Chip led Belle and Phillipe to a huge bathtub sitting in the middle of a terrace.

"Go on!" Chip told Phillipe. "Get in!"

Belle scrubbed the horse with a giant brush while Chip yelled encouragement.

"Look at all the bubbles! Try splashing around! Isn't this fun?"

Phillipe just sat there. When the bath was over he was squeaky clean—but still very sad.

By now Belle was very worried. What was wrong with poor Phillipe? She went to the castle library and pulled down every book about horses.

"He doesn't seem to have a cold, or a toothache, or anything wrong with his hooves," Belle thought, reading descriptions of various illnesses. Then she read a section of a book that explained the importance of exercise.

"Maybe that's it!" Belle said. "Maybe all Phillipe needs is to get out and gallop in the fresh air!"

Belle changed into her riding clothes and went out to the stables. "Phillipe, you and I are going for a nice, long ride," Belle announced. "Won't that be nice?"

The horse seemed to perk up just a little bit as Belle saddled him up, and she was hopeful that the ride soon would have Phillipe back to his old self.

Belle rode Phillipe out into the countryside. After a while, the horse came to a complete stop, sniffed the air, and turned his head from side to side.

"What is it, boy?" Belle asked. "Are you looking for something?" Phillipe glanced back at Belle dejectedly, then slowly walked on.

"Oh, how I wish you could tell me what's wrong," Belle said with a sigh.

Then, suddenly, Phillipe's head shot up, his nostrils flared, and he took off at a gallop.

"Slow down, Phillipe!" cried Belle, holding tightly onto the reins. "What's the hurry?"

As they came up over a hill, Belle had her answer. There, frolicking in a clearing, was a group of horses.

"Oh, I see," said Belle, "you've found some new friends to play with."

Belle dismounted so that Phillipe could go off and join the others. She watched as he ignored the group and headed straight for a pretty mare.

"Colette!" exclaimed Belle as she recognized the horse she had loaned to her neighbor just a few days before. Phillipe and Colette had stalls next door to each other in the castle stables, and had struck up quite a friendship. Now Belle understood what was wrong with Phillipe. He was lovesick from missing Colette!

Phillipe approached Colette as if to say, "Remember me? I've been lonely without you!"

Colette whinnied softly and moved closer to Phillipe. Apparently, she had missed him, too!

Belle rode Phillipe to her neighbor's, with Colette following close behind. After Belle explained the situation, her neighbor understood completely why Colette had to return home that afternoon.

"Who are we to stand in the way of true love?" he said to Belle with a smile.

On the ride back to the castle, Phillipe and Colette didn't let each other out of sight for a moment. Belle laughed to herself as she thought of all the things she and her friends had done to try and cheer up Phillipe.

"I'm sorry I didn't know what was wrong," she said, patting her horse's side. "But at least that bubble bath made you smell pretty for your lady friend!"

That night as Phillipe and Colette settled into their cozy side-by-side stalls in the stable, Belle could see from their happy faces that they belonged together—and that just like she and the Prince, they would live happily ever after.